Animal Homes

Dona Herweck Rice

Squirrels live inside the trees.

Honey hives are for the bees.

Beavers live beside their dams.

Barns are good for baby lambs.

Burrows are a place for mice.

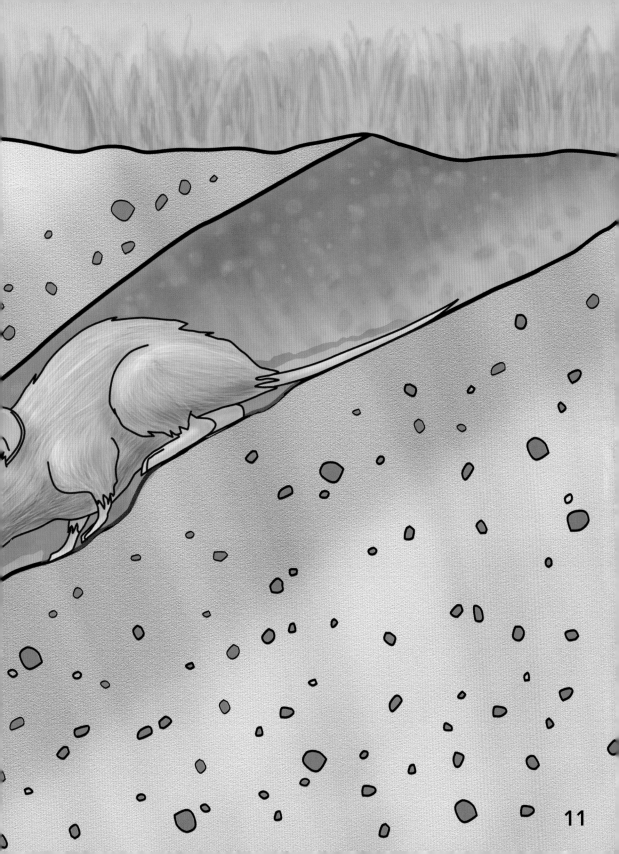

Lions think their caves are nice.

Dolphins live within the sea.

But houses are the place for me.